Alfred A. Knopf ⟋ New York

Buying, Training & Caring

YOUR for DINOSAUR

Written by
Laura Joy Rennert

Pictures by
Marc Brown

THIS IS A BORZOI BOOK PUBLISHED BY ALFRED A. KNOPF

Visit us on the Web! www.randomhouse.com/kids

Educators and librarians, for a variety of teaching tools,
visit us at www.randomhouse.com/teachers

Library of Congress Cataloging-in-Publication Data
Rennert, Laura.
Buying, training, and caring for your dinosaur / written by
Laura Joy Rennert ; illustrated by Marc Brown. — 1st ed.
        p. cm.
Summary: Includes instructions for choosing and caring for a pet dinosaur.
ISBN 978-0-375-83679-4 (trade) — ISBN 978-0-375-93679-1 (lib. bdg.)
[1. Dinosaurs—Fiction. 2. Pets—Fiction. 3. Humorous stories.]
I. Brown, Marc Tolon, ill. II. Title.
PZ7.R29025Bu 2009   [Fic]—dc22   2008050680

The text of this book is set in 20-point Blockhead Unplugged.
The illustrations in this book were created using a monoprint technique
with gouache where each image is painted in reverse on glass slowly adding
to the final textural surface.

MANUFACTURED IN CHINA
October 2009   10 9 8 7 6 5 4 3 2 1   First Edition

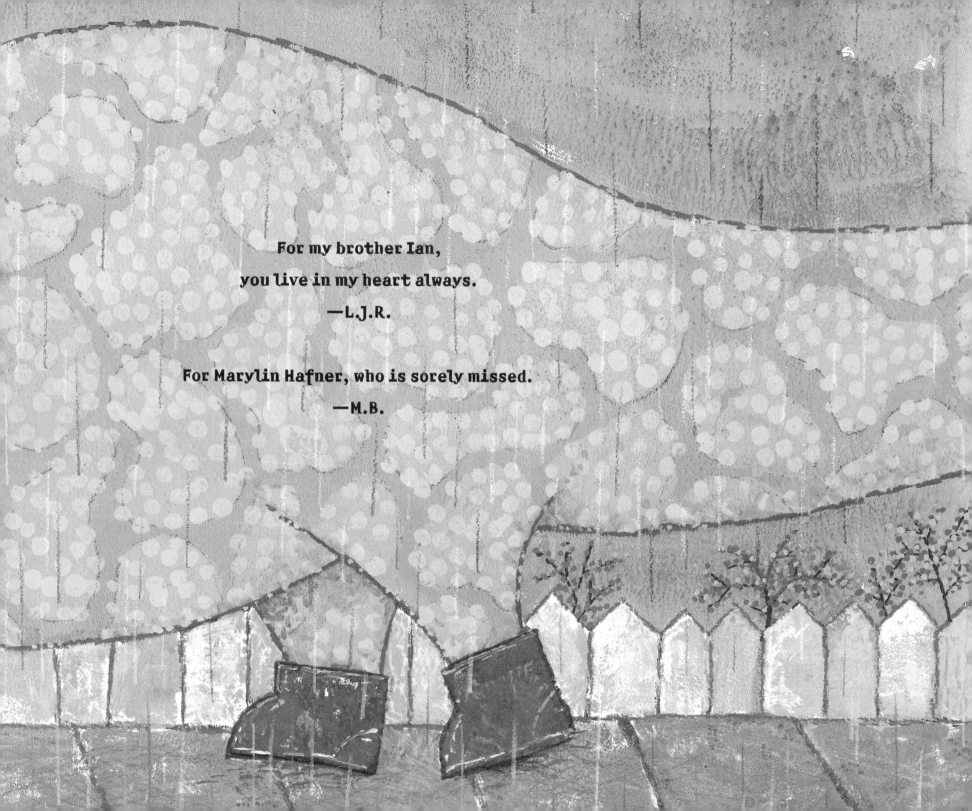

CHOOSING THE RIGHT DINOSAUR FOR YOU

There is a dino for every kid, and a kid for every dino. This guide will help you find the right one for you. Dinos make great pets, but some may need a little more housebreaking than others.

HORNED

Triceratops (try-SER-uh-tops)

With his bony frill and three horns, Triceratops is a great watch-dino. Please post a BEWARE OF DINO sign. Your mail carrier will appreciate this.

GINORMOUS

Diplodocus (dih-PLOD-uh-kus)

If bigger is better, then get a Diplodocus. Diplo will grow to be 90 feet long. Other kids have lemonade stands, but with Diplo, you can have your own roller coaster. Right in the front yard. Of the whole neighborhood.

Four legs the size of columns for shelter from wind, rain, snow, or sun.

Small head so that even though you can't let Diplo sleep in your bed (Mom's rules), she can rest her head on your pillow once the lights are out.

WINGED

PTERANODON (tuh-RA-nuh-don)

If you love sports, Pteranodon is the one for you. With Pterie by your side, you'll catch fly balls in the stands at baseball games and you'll always have the best seat in the house.

Long fourth finger perfect for removing unnecessary broccoli from dinner plates.

Wings make a great extra blanket on cold nights and a hammock when you want to sleep under the stars on camping trips.

SPINY

Spinosaurus (SPINE-uh-SAWR-us)

Although she's the perfect buddy all year round, Spinosaurus is a great warm-weather dino. On hot summer days, you can sit in the shade of Spiny's sail, drinking lemonade with your friends.

Long tail for shooing flies OR pesky sisters.

Bony sail means Spiny makes
an excellent sailboat.

SHARP-TOOTHED

Tyrannosaurus rex (ty-RAN-uh-SAWR-us REX)

If you bring this dino home, be sure you have a sturdy leash. Obedience school is a must! It is difficult to get **T.** rex under voice command. We're not sure where his ears are, if he HAS ears, because no one has gotten close enough to check.

Large, stiff tail to balance the weight of his huge head and his (did we mention?) gigantic teeth.

Itty-bitty arms—we don't know what they're for but are glad there's SOMETHING little about him.

BIG (and we do mean BIG) teeth—the better to grin with, we hope!

STARTING OFF RIGHT

You're ready to go to the pet store to get your new dino. Probably, Mom and Dad are out and cool Aunt Judy is babysitting. What do you need to bring Dino home?

1. You need a long, LOOOOOOOOOOOOOONG leash. We should probably add a strong, STROOOOOOOOOOOOOONG leash.

3. Definitely get something to cover the couch. In fact, it might not be a bad idea to cover the whole living room.

2. Be sure to buy LOTS of dino food.

4. Make Dino a soft, inviting bed of her own so she doesn't try to sleep in yours.

TEACHING AN OLD DINO NEW TRICKS

Your "new" dino has been around for millions of years. Some of his habits may be hard to change. But you can try.

SIT

Dinos tend to sit when **THEY** want to, not when **YOU** want them to. We recommend givin Dino a treat when he obeys. **NO**, you may not give your **T.** rex your little brother as a trea **YES**, do check under Dino **BEFORE** saying "Sit."

HEEL! STOP!

Dinos love to go for walks and will
stop when you tug on the leash.
Unfortunately, there are times
when Dino doesn't feel the tug. Like
when the neighbor's cat
races by. Or the neighbor's dog. Or
the neighbor's car. Oh, well.

STAY (Ha!)

YOU try telling a several-ton
dino that he has to wait nicely
for his dinner.

FETCH

Fetch is a game that instinctively appeals to many dinos. Dinos will run to retrieve a stick or ball. We recommend a stick because balls don't usually last very long. (Actually, neither do sticks.) Make sure you throw the stick or ball FAR AWAY from Dad's car.

ROLL OVER

Let's not even GO there.

FEEDING YOUR DINO

1. Feed Dino three meals a day.
2. PLUS snacks. You don't want Dino to be hungry when you put her in the backyard. With your sister's cat.
3. Dinos love fancy meals . . . so you might not want to leave Dino alone with the holiday buffet OR the Christmas tree.

BATHING YOUR DINO

1. Dress in clothes that you can get wet. VERY WET.

2. Have A LOT of soap, sponges, towels, and friends on hand. Especially since dinos can be VERY ticklish.

3. Some moms get unhappy when bathwater runs out of the bathtub. Into the hall. And down the stairs. If this sounds like your mom, take Dino to the car wash instead.

EXERCISING YOUR DINO

Most dinos need lots of exercise. If YOU ate a ton of food a day, you would too.

Sign Dino up for your soccer league. Dinos make especially good goalies.

Take Dino swimming. Dino makes a wonderful flotation device and water slide. Hey—who needs a diving board?

TAKING DINO TO SCHOOL

1. We recommend doing this only on days when you have show-and-tell. Dinos can be a bit distracting.
2. You should know that while dinos do seem to like library time, librarians DON'T always like dinos.

TAKING DINO TO THE VET

1. CALL AHEAD. Vets seem to prefer this.
2. DON'T tell Dino it's time for his shots. EVER!
3. Don't try to take Dino to the vet with only Mom.
We're guessing you'll want Dad and ... er ... maybe all
your aunts and uncles to help you.

TRAVELING WITH DINO

Dinos are very good travelers, and they love to go visit Grandma and Grandpa. But moving them from one place to another CAN be an issue.

BY PLANE

Buy extra seats. LOTS of extra seats. Or charter a Quetzalcoatlus (KET-sol-koh-AT-lus). Sometimes it's good to have wings that are 35 feet long.

BY CAR

Make sure to leave the windows open. Extra leg room or, in this case, head and tail room is always good.

BY OTHER MEANS

Help the environment by saving gas.
Drive DINO and leave the car at home.
Going through the drive-through can be
a bit of a challenge, though.

QUICK BURGER

DRIVE THRU

The nice thing about Dino is that being away from home is never
lonely when he is there.

Now that you know how to buy, train, and care for your dinosaur,
let's get to the most important thing.

DINOS ARE

FOR FUN!

Dinos LOVE to have their bellies rubbed. We recommend making sure there is lots of room for a good belly rubbing before beginning.

Like any pet, Dino mostly wants lots of
TLC—tender loving care. A little chocolate
now and then doesn't hurt either.

They also love to cuddle. Be sure
to pet their snouts, heads, and
crests and to scratch behind their
ears (er ... wherever they are).

And most of all, HUG your
dino (okay ... part of
your dino) every day.

So enjoy your new pet, and never forget that
A DINO IS A KID'S BEST FRIEND!

HELPFUL RECOMMENDATIONS

Suited to city life: Compsognathus (komp-SOG-nuh-thus)

Good with children: Iguanodon (ih-GWON-uh-don),

  Brachiosaurus (BRAY-key-uh-SAWR-us)

Good watch-dino: Triceratops, T. rex

Exercise necessary: Gallimimus (GAL-ih-MIME-us)

Difficult to groom: Ankylosaurus (AN-kuh-luh-SAWR-us), Spinosaurus

Needs a big backyard: Diplodocus

Hard to train (pea brain): Stegosaurus (STEG-uh-SAWR-us)

Easy to train (biggest brain): Troodon (TROH-uh-don)

Potential health problems: Extinction, but not for millions of years . . .